MOOSE MUSIC

For all little learner musicians, but especially for their Mothers.

And for Becky and Jo Wignell,
Rebecca Markless, Joanna Pace and
David and Megan Porter.

First published in hardback in Great Britain
by HarperCollins Publishers Ltd in 1994
First published in Picture Lions in 1995
10 9 8 7 6 5 4 3 2 1
Picture Lions is an imprint of the Children's Division,
part of HarperCollins Publishers Ltd
Text and illustrations copyright © Sue Porter 1994
Designed in conjunction with Sue Porter
The author asserts the moral right to be
identified as the author of the work.
ISBN 0 00 664566-6

Printed and bound in Hong Kong

MOOSE MUSIC

Sue Porter

PictureLions
An Imprint of HarperCollins*Publishers*

Moose was walking in the woods, when he came across a mudpool. There, sticking out of the mud, was an old fiddle.

"Fantastic!" Moose said and pounced on it. He drew the bow across the rusty strings. This made a dreadful, ear-splitting screech which rattled all the leaves on all the trees for miles around.

"Lovely," said Moose.

Down river, the beavers were building a dam.
"Come on everyone," called Father Beaver,
"one last, big effort. **HEAVE!**"

sCrRREEEECHH! went the fiddle.

CRRAAASHH! went the dam.
"Get that moose away from here!"
yelled Father Beaver.

But Moose had already gone.

Bear was busy stealing honey. He stretched out his paw as far as he could towards the nest.

sCRREEECHH! went the fiddle.

CRRAAASHH! went Bear.
"Take that diabolical instrument elsewhere!"
he shouted.

Moose didn't wait to be told twice.

Pierre was cutting down trees. They always fell just where he wanted.

sCRREEECHH! went the fiddle.

CRRAAASHH! went the tree.
"Come back here!" shouted Pierre.

But Moose thought he'd better not.

Moose sat on a log and hung his head.
"It seems that no one around here appreciates good music," he said. And he got up and plodded sadly off into the forest.

At last he came to a lonely place. He watched
the sun slowly sinking. Lifting his fiddle, he
began to play with all his heart.

"What lovely music," said a voice
from the trees.

"It makes me feel like singing," said
the lady moose.

"Please go ahead," said Moose.

The grating of her voice was every bit as horrible as Moose's fiddle. It rasped and howled and echoed around the lakes and mountains.

Moose gasped. His ears shook. His eyes bulged. He quivered all over. It was just the sort of sound that mooses really like.

Moose was in love.

"Lovely," he said, "let's do it, let's make moose music."